Cross-Stripe

A Christmas Miracle on Route 66

Written & Illustrated

by

Cheryl M. Gower

Cross-Stripe: A Christmas Miracle on Route 66

Copyright © 2008 by Cheryl M. Gower

ISBN 978-1-60643-797-1

Library of Congress Control Number: 2009903577

Published by: Gowergraphics, Fort Mohave, Arizona

Second Printing

All rights reserved. No part of this book may be reproduced or transmitted in any form or by any means without written permission of the author.

Printed in the United States of America

Other books by this author:

Cross-Stripe: Bolt And The Bed Races

    ISBN 978-1-61539-275-9

This book is dedicated to

My loving husband, Jim,

for his never-ending

support and encouragement

Table of Contents

Chapter One ~ Christmas Plans.......................1

Chapter Two ~ Bolt and Rooter......................4

Chapter Three ~ The Christmas Parade................6

Chapter Four ~ The Wreck..........................11

Chapter Five ~ The Rescue.........................14

Chapter Six ~ A Night in the Stable..................19

Chapter Seven ~ Off to the Hospital..................29

Chapter Eight ~ Bolt's Miracle......................31

Chapter Nine ~ Rooter's Miracle....................35

Legend of the Burro's Cross-Stripe....................39
Word Helper.......................................40
Reading for Understanding.........................43
Author's Notes....................................44
Your Notes..45

Acknowledgments

The People of Oatman, Arizona, especially
    Jackie Rowland, Fast Fannie's Souvenirs
    Ellen DeLong, Ocotillo Gallery & Framing
    Tom & Jennifer McCarthy, Oatman Stables
    Oatman Volunteer Firefighters & EMTs

Tennessee Donkey ASSociation
    Lydia Spears, Pres.

The Great American Press
    Victor, Joel, Ann Marie and Staff

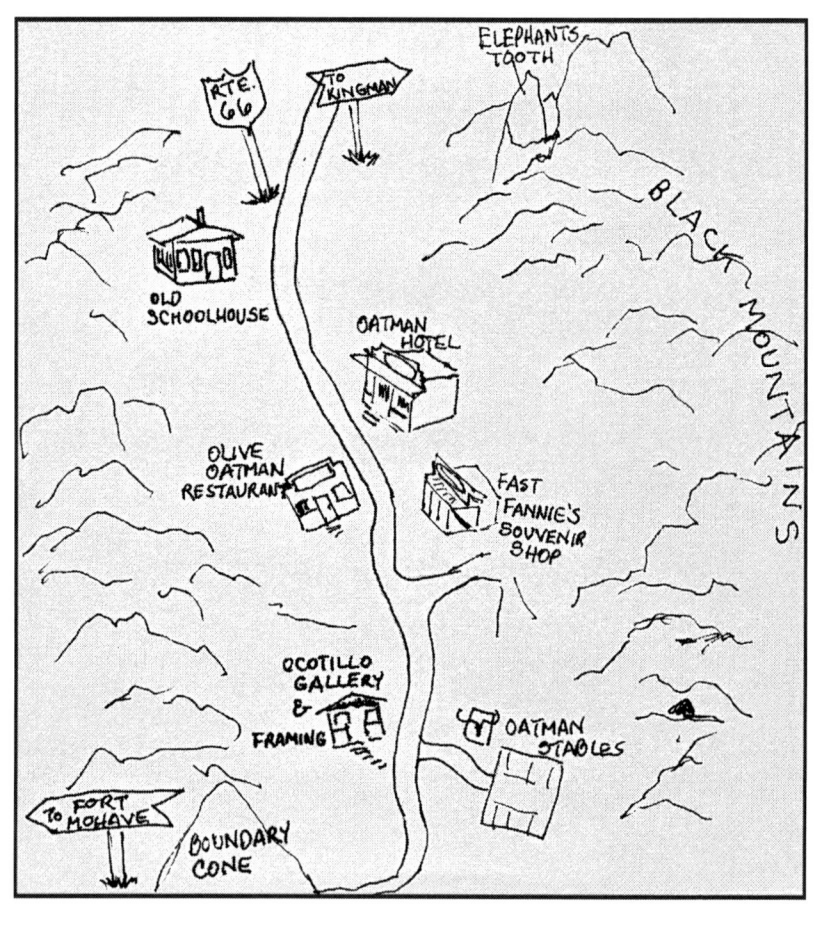

Map of Oatman, Arizona
as it applies to this story

Chapter One ~ Christmas Plans

"Have you made any plans for Christmas?"

"Not weally," replied Rooter as he aimlessly kicked a pebble down the hillside path. He and his buddy, Bolt, often explored the many trails that zigzag through the mountains surrounding Oatman, Arizona. The recent winter showers brought new grasses to life and the brittlebush's soft shoots provided tasty treats for a little burro's and javelina's lunch.

Between nibbles, Bolt flicked his long ears and mumbled, "I was sort of hoping we could do something different this year, something to make the holiday special." His thoughts drifted to past Christmases—going from cabin to trailer braying for treats and handouts, or watching the Oatman residents select mesquite shrubs along Route 66 and hang all sorts of shiny brick-a-brack and stringy tinsel on the branches. One year a red ball caught Rooter's eye. Expecting the sweet juicy crunch when he bit into a ripe prickly pear, he squealed in pain as the red ball shattered and badly cut his snout, leaving a disfiguring scar. Most of his javelina [pronounced hav-a-lee-na] family and friends had abandoned him because of his ugly face. When Rooter spoke, they teased him saying, "We can't understand a word you say!"

But Bolt, an orphaned burro, and somewhat stunted due to the lack of his mother's milk in his early months, knew how it felt to be avoided by one's own. As if his size weren't enough to embarrass him in the eyes of his herd, Bolt was born without the hereditary spinal stripe and shoulder cross-stripe. He was the laughing stock of his family. As much as he missed his mother, Bolt was glad she didn't have to suffer from their loud, lip-curling, abuse. It is legend that because the burro was employed to carry Jesus through the crowds on Palm Sunday, the burro and all his future offspring were blessed with the sign of

Chapter One Christmas Plans

the Cross for his service. And as the burro walked through a layer of palm branches, they brushed his legs and left their marks. No one knew why Bolt didn't have this cross-shaped stripe and leg stripes. All of the others in his herd showed their stripes.

Chapter Two ~ Bolt and Rooter

Bolt and Rooter's unlikely friendship began when Bolt discovered Rooter wandering in Silver Creek Wash. Rooter seemed weak and dazed. Bolt knew immediately that the little peccary needed water or he would soon pass out and die. The watering hole was too far away and Rooter would never make the climb. To bring some quick relief, Bolt pawed at a prickly pear cactus, breaking off a paddle or two. Very gingerly, he picked one up and dropped it in front of Rooter, whose snout could handle the stickers with ease. He chewed the cactus leaf with relish. Soon he seemed a bit revived and Bolt was able to lead him up the wash to a small pool of water hidden in a collection of granite boulders. His tiny hooves and Rooter's cloven feet picked their way sure-footedly up and down the narrow, winding trails, finally arriving at the rain collection spot.

After sipping what seemed to be gallons of water from the tiny pool, Rooter looked shyly around him, catching sight of Bolt out of the corner of his eye. "Tank you for heppin' me. I m-m-musta lost my way." All the while he was speaking, Rooter hid the side of his face with

Chapter Two ~ Bolt and Rooter

the ugly scar. And his speech was affected by it too, making him a little difficult to understand.

Bolt reassured Rooter, "No trouble. You'd do the same. Do you feel like goin' down into town? It's about the usual time when the crowds gather. They love to hand out tasty carrots. Might be just what you need 'bout now."

Rooter looked with surprise at the little burro, stunned by Bolt's suggestion. *Why isn't he running away from me and my ugly face like all the others? And why would he want to be seen in public with me?*

"Hey, Bolt, as g-g-good as doze cawuts sound…"

Before Rooter could finish, and sensing the reason for his hesitancy, Bolt put his ears back and brayed at the little pig, "I accept you as my friend no matter what you look like, how you sound, or for that matter, how you smell. What others think makes no difference to me. So come on. My stomach's aching for some carrots. Yum!"

From that day on, Bolt and Rooter were nearly inseparable. Even when Sadie, a rather aggressive burro, challenged Rooter's presence, Bolt was right there to give her a swift side kick and nip her haunch. The rest of the herd got the message and seemed to tolerate Rooter's claim to some of the tasty fare served up by the town's tourists.

"I guess we're just going to have to be satisfied with a same-old, same-old Christmas," Bolt sighed.

Chapter Three ~ The Christmas Parade

Once their bellies were full from all the ready handouts, the two friends started up the uneven pavement, the same well-worn trail from the west coast to Chicago early travelers in stagecoaches and autos called Route 66. Plodding up the hill toward the old, boarded-up schoolhouse, Bolt and Rooter heard all sorts of noise coming from that direction. There was daily traffic on this road, but the engines and horns, people hollering and cheering was a little out of the ordinary. Suddenly Zip the roadrunner passed them in his usual flurry, crying, "Eek! Eek! Gotta run! Gotta run!"

Chapter Three ~ The Christmas Parade

Wondering what could have set his tail feathers on fire, Bolt and Rooter looked back up the street to see a huge fire engine coming at them with siren whining. A 1902 Model-T followed close behind, bulging with people throwing wrapped candies to the cheering crowds along the street. Wild West gunmen shot their pistols in the air, hooting and hollering as if they had just scored a rich bank robbery. The burro and javelina had seen enough! Giving each other a wide-eyed look, they turned tail and made a fast exit to the south end of town, past the Oatman Hotel and Fast Fannie's, down a side street beyond the old mine and up an embankment to safer ground. With their breath coming out in quick puffs, the animals watched the display rumble past. At the end of the parade was an old hay wagon carrying a chubby man with a white beard and rosy cheeks in a red suit and hat. He was waving and smiling to everyone, wishing them a Merry Christmas and a Ho-Ho-Ho.

Bolt snorted and tossing his head said, "I completely forgot! Today's the Oatman Christmas Parade. No wonder so many people are here."

Rooter looked at his friend. "What are you t-t-talking aboud?" Even though Bolt and Rooter had been friends for a few years, this was the first time Rooter had come to Oatman at Christmastime. His usually spent most of his time in Golden Valley, where he loved to root up tasty plant bulbs and grasses to eat. However, this year there seemed to be more hunters roaming the valley, so Rooter made his way up the Black Mountains, where he would be safe in the company of his buddy, Bolt. And just when he thought he'd escaped the hunters' bullets, he walked right into a bunch of crazy cowboys dancing around and firing their pistols into the air.

Chapter Three ~ The Christmas Parade

"I'm talking about parades like this, decorations, lots of happy people visiting and bringing treats. Everyone in town goes all out to welcome them. It's very exciting as you just saw," he assured his friend. "But I'd still like to do something really special--something to make this Christmas memorable--maybe do something for someone else. Think! Is there something we could do?"

"I can't tink ob anyting right n-n-now, but maybe we c-c-could head on back to the center of town, where da crowd seems to be having a good time, and we'll c-c-come up wit an idea."

So the two pals ambled up the street, stopping at a shop on one side, a restaurant on the other, accepting carrots, hay and oats from the happy throng. The sun was beginning to set behind the mountains, casting brilliant hues of purple, coral red and gold on the rocky cliffs. Soon the noisy crowds would head for their cars and a sweet hush would descend on the little mining town once again. That was a signal for Bolt and Rooter to find a cozy niche to settle down for the night, preferably one whose rocks had been warmed by the sun.

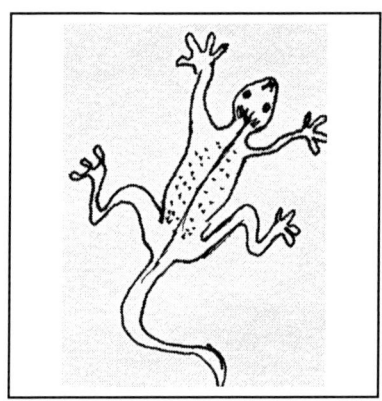

Chapter Four ~ The Wreck

The two buddies barely drifted off to sleep when, from far down the curvy, well-worn highway came the sound of clanking, crunching metal and the steady blaring of a car horn. The night sky was dappled with brilliant flecks of light, but no moon. Glancing in the direction of the loud--and annoying--sound, Rooter followed Bolt (peccaries' eyesight isn't very good) at a slow trot to see what was making all the noise. Carefully picking their way through the mesquite and sage, the pair came upon a car off the side of the road, just across from the Ocotillo Gallery & Frame Shop, where the light from the porch somewhat illuminated the wreck. Steam rose from the front end, making a hissing sound just like a snake. And snakes were not among Bolt or Rooter's favorite things. They halted, afraid that the hissing would be quickly followed by the strike of a desert rattler.

Realizing the hissing was not a snake, Bolt cautiously walked around the side of the auto and peered into the side window. All he could see were big, white billowy things.

"That's strange," he whispered to Rooter, "Usually there are people in these contraptions, just like in the parade."

Something moved inside. The billowy white thing collapsed and a man's groggy face appeared from the other side of the window. He was as startled to see a burro's muzzle pressed against the glass as Bolt was when the window rolled down! Bolt jumped back, eyes as big as golf balls, and nearly as white!

By this time Rooter had scampered back up to the side of the road but not before the man gasped and said, "Whew! Is there a skunk around here?" Bolt glanced over his shoulder at Rooter, who hung his head in shame. He felt sad that his little friend offended everyone with his smell—everyone but him. Bolt had learned that if he nuzzled in a sage bush and got the pungent scent all over his muzzle and in his nostrils, he didn't much mind Rooter's odor. After all, Rooter couldn't help it. That's just the way peccaries are. And friends overlook each other's flaws.

A moan caught Bolt's attention. The man's unsteady gaze turned toward the person sitting next to him. A young woman began to stir, but was restricted by another big white pillow and her seatbelt.

"MaryAnne, are you all right?"

Chapter Four ~ The Wreck

"Oh, Joe, what happened?" MaryAnne said groggily. "Yes, I think I'm okay. How about you, dear?" And then she screamed.

Bolt jumped again, his heart thumping. These people act like they've never seen a donkey before! Just then he heard the crunch of gravel from the road above the car.

"What's all the ruckus? My glory, a soul can't get a bit of work done, much less enjoy a lick of peace up…" Before she could finish, Ellen clapped a hand over her mouth. "Well, I declare! What have we here?" she asked, raising her lantern so she could get a better view of the teetering, battered, hissing vehicle. Ellen had lived in Oatman for nearly twenty years. She knew these narrow, winding roads could be treacherous in daylight, let alone on a dark, wintry night. Accidents were frequent occurrences here.

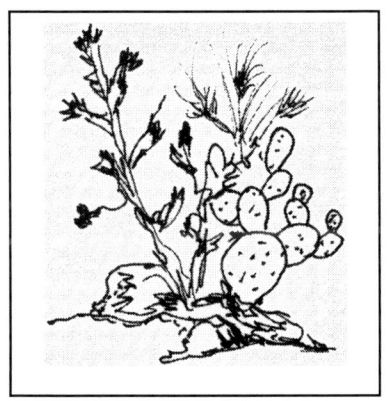

Chapter Five ~ The Rescue

"Bolt, did you cause this?" she asked, knowing the burros had learned that by standing in the road, cars and trucks loaded with people would stop and hand out tasty delights not found naturally in the desert, but nonetheless very appreciated.

"Hey, miss! Glad you came along," Joe stammered. "I guess I was going a little too fast to manage these curves on a dark night like this. My wife…pregnant…maybe needs help," he slurred, as he struggled to remain conscious. Reaching over, he gave his wife's hand a loving squeeze.

"Oh, my!" Ellen cried, "We better get you some help, and fast!"

All the while, Bolt and Rooter looked on with increasing interest. Ellen tugged on the driver's door, but it was jammed against a rock. Climbing down to the passenger's side, she was able to get MaryAnne to unlock her door. It swung open with a creak and a thud.

"Bolt!" Ellen called. "Come on, Bolt. Get over here and earn your keep. We gotta get this young mother-to-be somewhere safe, so she can rest."

Chapter Five ~ The Rescue

In all the commotion, Zip appeared out of nowhere, probably aroused from sleep in a nearby mesquite tree. "Eek! What's shakin'? Eek!" Darting here and there, jumping to the hood of the car and down again, Zip ran circles around the mangled auto, adding more chaos to the situation.

Ellen took charge, spreading her buckskin jacket over Bolt's back and gently helping MaryAnne aboard the strong little burro. The petite lady sat comfortably sidesaddle, and gripped the short, bristly mane to steady herself. Ellen helped Joe slide across the seat and out the passenger door. The brisk night air seemed to revive him and he was able to walk alongside the burro and his wife, making sure she didn't fall off.

"Zip, run ahead and make sure they have a room at the Oatman Hotel." At Ellen's command, Zip raced up the road, chattering all the way.

Ellen removed her belt, looped it around Bolt's neck and began leading the sure-footed beast up out of the ravine and back onto the road. Rooter followed at a distance, even though he was downwind of the rescued couple. One cautious step after another, the little troupe scaled the uncertain ledges until they reached the pavement of Route 66. Joe did his best to keep his wits about him, wrapping a loving arm around his wife. MaryAnne let out a groan as another labor pain gripped her heavy abdomen.

"Is everything all right?" Joe asked, much concern in his voice. "We'll be at the hotel soon, and we can get you into a nice comfy bed. Hang in there a little longer." He realized that this was the most involved he'd been in MaryAnne's entire pregnancy. It was now that he regretted putting off reading some of the books on birthing and childcare his wife brought home from each doctor visit.

Ellen urged Bolt a little faster, now that they were on the roadway. Just when the hotel lights came into view, Zip seemed to appear out of nowhere.

Chapter Five ~ The Rescue

"Eek! No room, no room! Eek!" he cackled, flicking his tail one way then the other. Bolt stopped dead in his tracks. *What are we going to do now? How will I get Ellen to understand?* he thought. She pulled and tugged on the belt, but Bolt refused to budge. She yanked and pleaded. Nothing seemed to influence the little burro to move—not even when Ellen tempted him with a carrot left in her jacket pocket from earlier in the day.

"Bolt's tryin' to tell us somethin'," she drawled. "Okay, Bolt, you seem to have a better idea, or are you warning us of some danger we can't see?" she asked, moving her lantern left and right to check for any sign of trouble lurking in the dark. "You take us where you think we should go. Go on!" She dropped her grip on the belt and gave Bolt a firm pat on his rump.

Bolt took a big drink of the night air and started walking up the road a little farther before turning off to the right and up a rutted, gravel driveway. Joe encouraged MaryAnne with his soothing voice as another gasping groan escaped her lips.

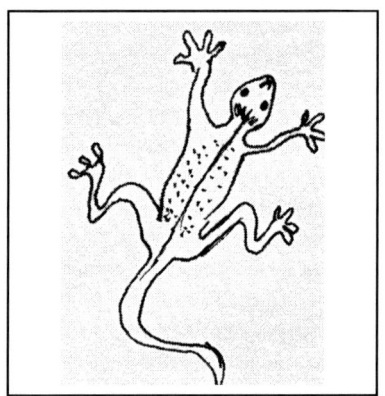

Chapter Six ~ A Night in the Stable

By this time, Ellen realized where the little burro was taking them. How smart of him. These burros never ceased to amaze her with their powers of observation and instinct. Bolt led the rescue party through the gate of the Oatman Stables. Tom and Jennie McCarthy had worked day and night building the barn and resting shed to establish their unique trail ride and barbeque business. He plodded past the watering trough and head-butted the barn door until Ellen gave him a hand. The fresh, sweet smell of alfalfa hay filled their nostrils. The trail ride horses looked up in amazement from their stalls. A burro had never been in the barn before, much less a javelina and a roadrunner. Plodding to the back of the barn, Bolt stopped at a space used to store fresh hay and straw. Ellen hung her lantern high on a nail to illuminate the stall with a warm glow. She grabbed several saddle blankets and spread them over the fluffy straw.

"Here," she said, "MaryAnne should be quite comfortable here! I'll see if I can find some more blankets. And you're both probably quite thirsty. How's that ankle of yours, Joe?"

"I'll be fine. I'm more concerned about MaryAnne's comfort and condition right now. If it swells up or turns another shade of purple, I'll have the paramedics look at it. But thanks for asking."

Joe helped MaryAnne from Bolt's back to the makeshift bed on the stable floor, while Ellen grabbed a bale hook and gaffed one bale after another until she had moved them around and stacked them to enclose the stall, not only for privacy, but to contain the warmth for MaryAnne and her expected child.

Quickly scrawling a note, Ellen called out, "Zip, take Rooter and go up to Tom and Jennie's house. Here, take this note. They'll know what to do." She put the paper in Zip's beak.

"Bolt, you stay in there with MaryAnne and Joe. Between the two of you, she should be plenty warm until help arrives." She pulled the heavy barn door closed after Zip and Rooter hurried off in the direction of the house. Nights were unusually chilly this year. Ellen puffed her warm breath on her hands, rubbed them briskly together, and hurried back to plug a few drafty holes with anything she could find.

Chapter Six ~ A Night in the Stable

Zip and Rooter hopped up on the front porch of Tom and Jennie's log and stone cabin. Twinkling lights from a small Christmas tree were the only evidence anyone was home. Zip gave the front door a few pecks. When he received no response, he hopped up on the windowsill, gave the pane of glass several forceful taps, and let out a chattery shriek. When he saw someone approaching from inside, he ran back to the door and waited.

Jennie peered out the window. Seeing no one, she turned to head back to her office, when she heard several more taps at the door. Opening it cautiously, she looked around, but didn't notice the messengers until Zip gave a little tail flick. Jennie looked down and to her surprise there was a roadrunner with a piece of paper in his beak. *But what is that foul smell?* she wondered.

"What's this?" she asked aloud. Quickly reading the note, she called to her husband, "Tom, get the portable heater out of the closet and get down to the barn. Ellen needs our help." Hurrying through the house, Jennie grabbed an armload of towels; filled a bucket with hot water; heaped fruit, nuts, carrots, bananas and some beef jerky in a bag; filled a thermos with drinking water; found her flashlight and loaded everything in her farm wagon. Rummaging through the hall closet, she found more blankets and a pillow. On her way out the door, she picked up some matches and incense sticks. With water pail in one hand, she pulled her Red Flyer farm wagon as fast as she could toward the barn. The stars seemed so close and bright in the Oatman sky. Even with no moon, they seemed to light her way.

Ellen heard the wagon's approach and opened the heavy door. "I'm so glad you were home tonight. They're back here. Not sure how far along she is, but it's their first child. Where's Tom?"

"He's getting our portable heater. It's pretty chilly tonight, and we can't have a new baby catching a cold," Jennie said. "Here are some towels and hot water. Oh,

Chapter Six ~ A Night in the Stable

and maybe the husband could use a little energy snack about now." Seeing Bolt dutifully performing his heat-providing assignment, Jennie offered him a carrot and patted him on the head.

Ellen introduced Joe to Jennie. "Pleased to meetcha," she said, giving his hand a firm shake. "How's your wife doing? Here's some drinking water for the two of you."

Joe looked back at MaryAnne, who had drifted off between contractions. "She's a real trouper. Even though this is our first child, she seems calm and confident—like she's done this many times already. Thank you for accommodating us like this. Your hospitality is mighty nice." Looking at his wife, he continued, "As long as Bolt, Zip and Rooter are here, there's probably time for you to go back to the house, warm up and get some supper. We'll be fine."

Jennie and Ellen looked at each other and agreed to go, provided Joe would send Zip up to the house as soon as they were needed. With Joe's promise, they left, but not before Jennie lit an incense stick—to camouflage some of Rooter's odoriferous scent. They met Tom just as he was arriving. He plugged the heater into a socket, made sure there was nothing nearby that could catch fire and headed back to the house for some of Jennie's homemade beef stew and buttermilk biscuits.

Rooter and Zip sidled closer to the stall where Bolt snoozed next to MaryAnne. Joe sat on a nearby bale munching on the snacks Jennie gave him. He held out an apple for Rooter, who took it and rolled it around on the barn floor before taking a hearty chomp out of it. Joe offered Zip some seeds and nuts, but the roadrunner didn't seem interested. He'd probably satisfy his hunger on some of the many spiders and mice that called the barn home.

Just then MaryAnne stirred, gasped and gave a little yelp. Joe immediately jumped up, dropping his snacks. Bolt rose to his feet, too. "MaryAnne, are you all right?" Joe asked solicitously.

"Joe, honey, I think it's time. But don't worry. Hand me some of those towels and put one in the bucket of water. Save one or two to wrap the baby." She gasped again and gave a few panting breaths.

The animals all moved out of the way, but stayed close enough to see what was happening. Their eyes grew wider watching and waiting, sensing that something truly special was about to happen. The trail ride horses nickered to each other, as if passing along the details of stall #9's activities.

"Zip," Joe called, "I just remembered. You're supposed to get Ellen and Jennie. I think it's time. Hurry, they'll know we need them when they see you. Now git!"

Chapter Six ~ A Night in the Stable

Joe opened the door and Zip made a dash for the cabin. Again, he regretted the fact that he hadn't taken a greater interest in the childbirth literature and classes MaryAnne suggested. He made a resolution that from now on, he'd take an active role in the parenting and care of this child. Nine months—seemed like there'd be plenty of time to learn the ropes of being a new dad. He'd enjoyed building the crib and changing table, and painting the nursery walls and helping MaryAnne hang the dotted Swiss curtains. Now it was showtime, and the stark reality was beginning to set in.

Joe looked out at the clear night sky. An especially brilliant star grabbed his attention and he spontaneously muttered a little prayer for the safety of his wife and new baby.

As he was putting all his weight into closing the barn door, he heard Jennie yell, "Wait up!" The three of them and Zip dashed inside, their cold breath streaming out behind them. "How's everything going?" Ellen asked.

The four walked quickly to the last stall. Bolt, Rooter and Zip looked from them to Mary Anne and back again. They all stood there in stunned silence and amazement. There was MaryAnne holding a tiny bundle, wrapped in terry towels. She looked up with the most glorious smile and welcomed them all to share in this wondrous moment. A rosy pink arm with five tiny fingers popped out of the toweling as if to greet his audience.

Joe knelt beside his wife and kissed the fuzzy head of his newborn son. "Mary Anne, what happened? I was only away for a moment…I didn't hear…how did you do this by yourself?" Joe's mystified expression brought a loving smile to his wife's face. She knew Joe hadn't paid much mind to the birthing part of having a child. She made sure she knew everything she needed to know, but never thought she'd deliver her child all by herself.

Chapter Six ~ A Night in the Stable

"Congratulations to the both of you!" Tom exclaimed. "We've had a few foals in here, but a human baby…this is a first. Consider yourself part of the family." Reaching into his sheep's wool jacket, Tom pulled out a shiny, gold nugget he had found in one of the old mines. "Please accept this as the little one's first birthday gift and a symbol of a rich life."

"Yes," Jennie agreed, "We are so happy for all three of you."

Ellen said, "We've called the paramedics and they should be here shortly. They can give you both a quick checkup and then transport you to Kingman Hospital, just to make sure everything is all right."

Tom asked, "What are you going to name the boy?"

MaryAnne looked at Joe and then to her smiling audience. "We've decided to name him Jesse. And because we will be eternally grateful for you and your hospitality, we would like to add Allen Joseph Thomas in your honor. God will bless all of you for your love and kindness."

Just then little Jesse Allen Joseph Thomas Christianson opened his mouth, took a deep breath and let out the loudest "Waah!" ever heard. Everyone burst out laughing. Pride shone on Joe's face as he took in the sight of his wife and son. Never did her think that he'd be welcoming his child into the world in a barn stall. But here he was on a cold desert night with a bunch of animals and strangers. Now they were good friends.

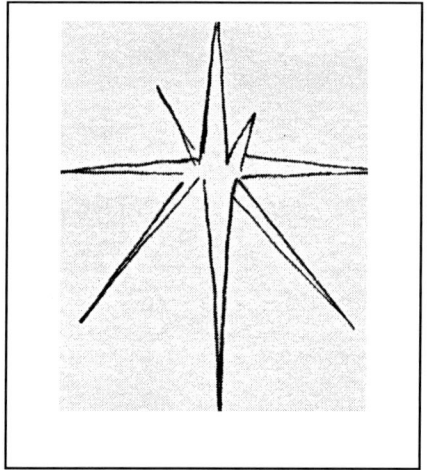

Chapter Seven ~ Off to the Hospital

Bolt's ears pricked up at attention. Zip hopped up on top of a stall divider and ran to the hayloft window. Rooter pranced around in circles. Off in the distance, the sirens of the Emergency Ambulance grew steadily louder. Tom waited at the barn door until he could see the backup lights through a knothole. He gave the door a heave and in rolled the rig. Out jumped Jim and Sherrie carrying their medical cases. Very efficiently, they went to work checking over both mother and child. They rolled out the gurney and first lifted MaryAnne onto it, then placed little Jesse in her outstretched arms.

Ellen and Jennie gave them a hug and wished them all the best. "Be sure to drop by on your way home. We want to keep in touch with our new 'nephew'."

Joe was invited to ride along in the ambulance, and he eagerly hopped in next to his new family. Before the rear doors drew shut, Tom reassured Joe that he and a few of the townsfolk would pull his car up to Andy's Garage and not to worry about it. With that, Joe shook Tom's hand and promised to let them know how everything panned out at the hospital. "Merry Christmas!" he yelled to the little group of people and animals.

Ellen, Jennie and Tom stood in the doorway until the lights of the ambulance disappeared around the curve at the bottom of the driveway. "Well, that was a lot of excitement for one night," Ellen sighed. "I think it's time I head for home. Thanks for all your help. You two have a very Merry Christmas."

Chapter 8 ~ Bolt's Miracle

"Ellen, let me drive you home," Tom offered. "Wouldn't want anything to happen to you, too."

"Oh pshaw, I'll be fine. I've got the lantern. And with the assistance of Bolt and Rooter, I shouldn't have any trouble. I'll just follow that star up there," she said pointing to an unusually brilliant heavenly body. "Come on, Bolt. Let's get outa here and let these good people get some sleep. Rooter, are you ready for a Christmas treat?" Swinging her kerosene lantern, Ellen, Bolt and Rooter made quite a trio picking their way down the rutted driveway. Zip had run off, probably back to his mesquite tree.

As they reached Ellen's place, her yard light made the lantern unnecessary. She was about to give Bolt a pat of affection and appreciation when she gasped in surprise. "Why, Bolt, what's this?" she asked, running her hand along his back. "Unless this light is casting odd shadows on you, I do believe there is a cross-stripe on your back! Where'd that come from?"

Bolt tried craning his neck to the right, then to the left. He turned around and around trying to catch a glimpse of this stripe. He looked like a dog chasing his tail!

Was Ellen right or just seeing things. "Rooter, can you see anything?"

Rooter ran from one side to the other, trying his best to see anything that looked like a stripe. He knew how much this would mean to Bolt. But his short little legs made it impossible to see, even if Bolt stood still for just a moment.

"Get up on that rock. Maybe you can get a better view," Bolt suggested. Rooter climbed up and Bolt moved next to the rock. Examining every inch of Bolt's shoulders and spine, Rooter finally declared, "Yep, yep, I think I uh…uh…see what Ellen's talking aboud. Sure wasn't dere befoh. We'll be able t-t-to see a lot betta tomowow, when da sun comes up. But foh n-n-now, if you can contain yoh

Chapter Eight ~ Bolt's Miracle

excitement, let's go get doze Cwistmas tweats Ellen mentioned."

Following Ellen to her back door, Bolt and Rooter relished the carrots that she gave them. She said, "Consider this my Christmas gift to you both. Everyone in town is going to be mighty amazed that you suddenly have your cross-stripe. They're going to ask how it happened. What shall we tell them?" She was silent for a moment, as if in meditative thought, when suddenly she exclaimed, "I think I have the answer! You are a descendant of the other donkey that carried Jesus, the one Mary rode into Bethlehem, led by Joseph. They had been ordered to return to their home town to be counted in the Roman census. And you even have new stripes on your legs! Oh, Bolt, you have been truly blessed for carrying MaryAnne and baby Jesse to the stable tonight."

The two listened to Ellen's soft voice as they munched contentedly on the crunchy vegetables. Her story made sense. They had a lot to think about. Once they finished, they made their way to their favorite spot to bed down for the night. Bolt's heart was dancing and his feet did their best to keep up with the beat. *This would really be something. Imagine, if it's true, what are the others going to say? How will we explain it?* he thought. Tonight would be the longest night of his life. First, the birth of baby Jesse, and now the possibility of getting his dearest wish. The anticipation was almost more than a little burro could endure. Falling asleep next to his best friend, Bolt's legs twitched and his eyelids flickered as visions of striped horses jumping over wide rivers and fat little pigs dancing in circles flashed in his restless dreams.

    Rooter nuzzled him, but Bolt just grunted and rolled over. Not until Rooter gave him a blunt jab with his snout did he open one eye and look around. The sky was turning a light blue, signaling the waking of a new day and lots of sunshine.

Chapter Nine ~ Rooter's Miracle

"Oh boy, Rooter! It's morning. Come on, get up. Whaddaya see? Whaddaya see?"

Rooter couldn't scramble to the top of the rock fast enough. Again he took a long hard look at Bolt's back. Finally, with great ceremony, Rooter was ready to make his pronouncement: "Yes, Bolt, my friend, you are now the proud owner of a dark stripe running from your shoulders to your rump and another crossing it at a ninety-degree angle at the shoulders. Yes, you have a cross-stripe."

Bolt stood there stock still. His lifelong wish had been granted. "It's a miracle!" he shouted. Jumping and bucking in a flurry of excitement, Bolt nearly fell head over hooves into a silver cholla cactus! "Wait a minute! Did my ears deceive me? You said I have a cross-stripe, and that truly is a miracle!" But Bolt wasn't just referring to <u>his</u> miracle. He went on, "Rooter, did you hear yourself just now?"

"What do you mean, Bolt? Of course, I heard myself. I'm not deaf! You have your stripe, and I'm very happy for you. It's a very good looking stripe and shows well on your blue-gray coat."

"No, no," Bolt responded, "I mean did you hear *how* you talked? You said every word correctly. No lisp; no stuttering. Look at me." Bolt examined Rooter's snout very carefully. Not once, but twice. Very calmly, so as not to alarm his friend, Bolt led Rooter to their crystal clear drinking pool. With a hushed tremor in his voice, he said, "Rooter, look at your reflection in the water."

Rooter lowered his head and peered into the still pool. After turning from side to side half a dozen times, he slowly raised his head, and with tearful eyes looked into the face of his best friend in the whole world. "Bo-o-olt," he asked slowly, "How did this happen?"

Chapter Nine ~ Rooter's Miracle

"I'm not sure, Rooter, but this Christmas has turned out to be *the* most special one ever. I wanted *us* to do something special and instead, something special was done *to us*."

Rooter agreed and added, "There are no treats that can compare to this Christmas gift, Bolt."

After much rejoicing and frolicking in the hills above Oatman, Bolt and Rooter met up with the rest of his herd. Bolt had a new swagger to his gait, and his blue-gray coat glistened with a special sheen. Rooter, no longer hanging his head and hiding his face, pranced along with his snout held high, sporting a warm smile instead of a sneering scar, and greeting everyone with a "Hi, howdie!!" The other burros, once quick to jeer and tease, immediately noticed the cross-stripe on Bolt's back. Sadie, the cantankerous female burro, found her way through the herd and showed signs of acceptance and flashed a look of fondness and admiration in his direction.

Rooter's face no longer disgusted or repulsed them. They could even understand what he said. His odor was still there, but somehow it didn't seem to annoy the others as much as it once had.

And of course, they had to go down to show Ellen, Tom and Jennie their new gifts. The people of Oatman were so proud of Bolt and Rooter. Every Christmas from then on, Bolt and Rooter led the parade down Route 66, and not even the sirens, horns, or popping pistols could keep them from their places in front of the fire engine, vintage cars and freshly polished emergency truck.

Rooter turned to his best friend in his little world and asked, "Any plans for Valentine's Day?"

Legend of the Burro's Cross-Stripe

The story is told that the little donkey that had been Jesus' mount on Palm Sunday came to the hill of Calvary. Seeing the tragic event occurring there, he wished with all his heart he had been able to carry the cross for Jesus, as he was the one to carry heavy burdens.

The donkey turned his back on the sight, but he could not leave because he wished to stay until all was over, out of his love for Jesus.

In reward for the loyal and humble love of the little donkey, the Lord caused the shadow of the cross to fall across his back and left it there for the donkey to carry forevermore as a sign that the love of God rewards the most humble act. It's also told that the leg stripes were received from walking through the palm branches that were laid in its path in honor of the sacred "burden" the donkey carried.

> Thanks to the website of the
> Tennessee Donkey ASSociation
> Lydia Spears, Pres.

Word Helper

This is a selection of words that younger children might have difficulty with pronunciation and meaning. The activities should be completed with the guidance of a parent or older sibling, or by themselves if they are capable. The pronunciation guides are phonetic rather than those given in a dictionary.

abdomen – (ab'-duh-men)noun, the part of a mammal between the ribs and hip area
accommodate – (uh-kom'-muh-date),verb, to do a service for; to supply with needs
billowy – (bil'-low-ee), adjective, to swell out as clouds or smoke
bray -- (bray), verb, the loud, harsh hee-haw sound made by a burro or donkey.
brilliant – (bril'-yunt), adjective, very bright, shining; very intelligent
census – (sen'-sus), noun, an official population count.
cloven –(klo'-vun), adjective, describing the split hoof of a pig or peccary.
collapse – (ko-laps'), verb, to fall down suddenly, or fold in on itself.
comply – (com-pli'), verb, to agree or yield to a command or wish.
conscious – (con'-shus), adjective, aware of your surroundings, senses; awake
contraption – (con-trap'-shun), noun, a bunch of things put together to make a sort of machine.
flaw – (flaw), noun, imperfection such as a scar, dent, scratch or character imperfection such as hate, jealousy, dishonesty.
gingerly – (jin'-jer-lee), adverb, cautiously, carefully.

hereditary – (her-ed'-i-tar-ee), adjective, passed down from one parent or ancestor to another through genes.
makeshift – (make'-shift), adjective, describing something put together as a temporary substitute for the real thing
meditative – (med'-i-ta-tiv), adjective, very deep in thought; pondering quietly
mesquite – (mes-keet'), noun, a thorny shrub or tree in the southwest USA and Mexico
niche – (nich or nesh), noun, an alcove or recess in a wall
nicker – (nik'-er), verb, the soft sound a horse makes through its nose and mouth
odoriferous – (oh-do-rif'-er-us), adjective, a strong, unpleasant smell
peccary – (pek'-a-ree), noun, a wild pig-like mammal; a javalina
ruckus – (ruk'-us), noun, a noisy disturbance
relish – (rel'-ish), verb, to enjoy
rummage – (rum'-ij), verb, to search thoroughly by turning over and disarranging things
shun – (shun), verb, to deliberately avoid or keep away from something out of hate
solicitously – (so-lis'-i-tus-lee), adverb, anxious and concerned; worried about another
stimulate – (sti'-mu-late), verb, to excite someone to get active
tolerate – (tall'-er-ate), verb, to respect the rights, opinions or practices of others; to put up with.
treacherous – (trech'-er-us), adjective, undependable; dangerous
whine – (wine), verb, a continuous high-pitched sound; to complain in a childish, irritating way.

Fun Vocabulary Ideas :

Use a word in a sentence, different from the way it was used in the story.

Try to use a new word each day in your conversation.

Find a word that means the opposite (antonym); or sounds alike (homonym).

Small rewards are great encouragement and make a game out of reading and learning, e.g. Stars or stickers on a chart; accumulate minutes for computer use, T.V. time, shopping monies, phone privilege time, etc. Preferably no food or sweets.

Reading for Understanding

1. Name three desert plants mentioned in the story.
2. What is the difference between Bolt's hooves and Rooter's?
3. If you were Bolt, who would be your Rooter? Why?
4. How is friendship shown between Bolt and Rooter?
5. The Oatman residents have two traditions mentioned in the story. What are they? What are some of your family's traditions?
6. How would you describe the people of Oatman?
7. What problems did Ellen come up against? How did she solve each of them?
8. What are some of Bolt's character traits that you admire?
9. What is another name for burro? What is another name for javelina?
10. What was Zip the roadrunner's main function (job) in the story? Why was he good at it?
11. What was the "billowy, white thing in Joe's car? What is the purpose of these devices?
12. Look at a map of Arizona. What is the next town northeast of Oatman on Route 66? Can you reach Phoenix on Route 66? Why or why not?
13. Why did Bolt get his stripe? Why was Rooter's snout healed?
14. What was the moral of the story—the lesson you learned from what happened to Bolt and Rooter because of their actions?
15. What was the symbolism in Tom's gold nugget gift to the baby?
16. Which meaning of the word "brilliant" was used in the story?
17. What do you think Bolt and Rooter might do for Valentine's Day?

Author's Notes

"*Cross-Stripe: A Christmas Miracle on Route 66*" is the latest venture in my professional writing experience. I use human and animal characters from our desert surroundings in an inviting story for children of all ages to learn about the geography, flora and fauna, character building traits, and the Christian legend as to how the burro inherited his stripes.

As a former educator, I recognize the need for reading challenge and improvement, which explains the reason for the included vocabulary and comprehension helps. Parents and older siblings can read the story aloud to younger children, encouraging them to build and advance their own vocabularies.

Look for the second in this series of stories with Bolt and Rooter, as they deal with friendship, jealousy and cooperation.
www.gowergraphics.net

Your Notes